TREE-
HOUSE
COMIX
Proudly
Presents

CAT KID
COMIC CLUB

WRITTEN AND ILLUSTRATED BY **DAV PILKEY**

AS GEORGE BEARD AND HAROLD HUTCHINS

WITH COLOR BY JOSE GARIBALDI

graphix

AN IMPRINT OF

■SCHOLASTIC

TO CLAIR FREDERICK AND THE MERRYMAKERS, INC. TEAM

Library of Congress Control Number 2020938611

978-1-338-71276-6 (POB)
978-1-338-71277-3 (Library)

10 9 8 7 6 5 4 3 2 1   20 21 22 23 24

Printed in China   62
First edition, December 2020

Edited by Ken Geist
Lettering and art by Dav Pilkey
Book design by Dav Pilkey and Phil Falco
Color by Jose Garibaldi
Color flatting by Aaron Polk
Publisher: David Saylor

CHAPTERS & COMICS

Hey, guys...

...Welcome to the **FiRST** meeting of...

...The CAT KiD COMIC CLUB!!!

HOORAY!!!

This is Li'l Petey! He's the President.

And **I'm** the **VICE PRESIDENT!**

How come **Molly** gets to be Vice President???

Yeah!

'CUZ I CALLED it FIRST. I GOT DIBS!!!

RATS!

NO FAIR!

OH! OH! OOH!!!

... and draw a line on your paper...

... like this.

Now on the **LEFT** side, write **Five** things you **Love**.

Pizza
BubbleGum
Squids
Videos
Katydids

Comics
Fireflies
Popcorn
Frien

Okay. Now on the other side...

...write five things ya like to **DO!!!**

Play
read
Laugh
Write
Draw

Actually, that's Pretty Good!!!

Now let's all try to think up an idea...

...by using stuff from Melvin's lists!

PLAY
read
Laugh
write
DRAW

He could write about a Dinosaur who likes to brush his teeth.

OR a nerd who likes to Annoy people.

Dennis the Toothbrush Who Wanted to be a Dinosaur Lawyer

By: Melvin the Frog

One time there was a
toothbrush...

... named Dennis...

... who wanted to be a
Lawyer.

For Dinosaurs.

So...

... Yeah.

The END.

About the Author

MeLvin the Frog

No BeLL
Peace
Prize For
Graphic Novels

Melvin the Frog is widely known as one of the world's most important Major voices in Graphic Literature.

He has won ~~TWO~~ countless Awards for his Genius and awesome humility.

His awesomeness has inspired countless ~~Ge~~ Generations and stuff.

COMING SOON:

Dennis the toothbrush Who Wanted to be a Dinosaur Lawyer 2: CRetaceous Court

Well, that was dumb.

HEY!

We DO **NOT** TALK TO EACH OTHER Like ThaT, NAOMI!

But I WAS just being **HONEST!**

DO YOU NeeD to Go SiT ON The TiME-OUT ROCK?

NO.

Then you need to Apologize to Melvin!

I'm sorry your comic was dumb.

TIME OUT.

PLay
read
Laugh
write
Draw

And So...

WORST DAY EVER!

Don't worry, Molly. Things will be better tomorrow!

How could they get any worse?

Chapter 2

We Quit!

Hey, guys. Welcome to day 2 of the Cat Kid Com— Excuse me, Molly.

Before you begin, Naomi has something she'd like to say.

Naomi?

Um... well... I...

I'm sorry I said your comic was dumb, Melvin.

You may continue, Molly.

Alright, guys. Does anybody want to share the comic they're working on?

Anybody?

Did **ANYBODY** work on their comic last night?

I couldn't think of any good ideas.

Me neither.

I'm not good at art.

Yeah. I can't draw good.

So **NOBODY** made a comic last night???

I tried, but it was dumb.

I ripped mine up.

I can't spell good.

Um — no offense, but me and Summer quit.

Yeah. No offense.

Why?

Comics just aren't our **Thing.**

Sorry, dude.

See ya Later.

WAiT!

What **IS** your **Thing?**

Summer likes photography.

And Starla is a **POET!**

Oh.

Well comics don't have to be <u>**STORIES!**</u>

They could be **Poems!**

LET'S GO!

I'll write some new HAIKU!

And I'll get my CAMERA!

And the **REST** of you...

...I'm **SO** DiSAPPOINTED!

FEAR! FEAR! FEAR!

If you guys want to be in this club...

...then you've got to get over your **FeaRS!**

So your assignment for tomorrow...

...is to **FAIL!**

Fail

They want us to **Fail?**

Yeah! BiG Time!

iL

Um— how?

Tonight I want you all to make a comic...

...that is **TERRIBLE!!!**

Yeah! Make a **SUPA DUMB** one!

EMBARRASS YOURSELF!!!

CHAPTER 3

FOUR FABULOUS FLOPS

MonsTer CHeese Sandwich

★ Story by: Naomi ★ Art by: Corky

★ Color by: Pink ★ Lettering by: Kendrick

Momma had a little baby.

Little Baby was very hungry.

I will make a muenster cheese sandwich for you

So she went to the fridge.

But Momma grabbed the wrong cheese by accident.

Momma cut the cheese.

43

46

HOW 2 DRAW

the Monster Cheese Sandwich

in 17 Ridiculously easy steps

Author's Notes:

Naomi
the
Great

"This story is based on the truth. One time Daddy said he was going to make us Muenster cheese sandwiches, but I thought he said 'Monster cheese sandwiches.' I got scared and cried (I was really little). Now we all call muenster cheese 'Monster cheese' because we think it's funny but it wasn't at first." —Naomi the Great

About the Illustrator:

corky

Corky has been an artist ever since he was a tadpole. His secret is to draw every day and don't give up even if you make lots of mistakes.

About the Colorist:

Pink

Pink loves music. He can play the ukulele pretty good. He also loves to sing and wrestle.

About the Letterer:

Kendrick

Kendrick the Frog is an awesome Dude. ~~when~~ He likes swimming and collecting stickers. When he is big, he will stay up as late as he wants.

That was **AWESOME!**

But I thought you were supposed to make a **BAD** comic!

Molly said it could be **DUMB**!

Yeeeeah. But it's still **AWESOME.**

Really?

I think you failed at **FAILING**, dude.

Aw, maaan!!!

Did you like it, Daddy?

Yes! But the ending was a little violent, don't you think?

Yeah! It was **TOTALLY** violent!

Okay, who's next?

Me! Me! Me!

MY DOG

by Pedro

54

MY DOG Saved the World.

The END.

About the Author and Illustrator

Pedro

Pedro is nice.
P.S. This story wasn't true. It is Fake. Pedro really doesn't have a dog but he wants one but Daddy says no every time but maybe I will some day when I am responsible.

The End.

HOW 2 DRAW

MY DOG'S POOPS

in 3 ridonculously easy steps

① ② ③

now Give my DOG'S poops some personality:

eyes   smile   happy   sad   sleepy

Robot Poop   Bad guy Poop   Baby Poop   Lady Poop   Ninja Poop

Pirate Poop   mummy Poop   Cyclops Poop   Betty Poop   winnie the Poop

Spider Poop   Bat Poop   Poobacca   Boba Poop   Storm-Pooper

That was **AWESOME**, Pedro!!!

Yeah! Good Job!!!

Yes, that was very good, Pedro!

...but the potty humor wasn't necessary, was it?

That was my favorite part!

I DO NOT WANT YOU KIDS WRITING POOP JOKES!

Why?

Because there is **NOThinG** funny About **Poo-Poo!!!**

HA HA HA HA HA HA HA HA

Did **Anyone** make a comic that **ISN'T VIOLENT OR DISGUSTING?**

We Did!!!

Our comic is 100% free of offensiveness!

SUPA FAIL

F

BY K.T., Kip, and Curly

and so...

Gee, Thanks for Destroying the Earth.

But Look! I saved your toothpick!!

HOORAY FOR SUPA FAiL!

The End!

Coming Soon:
Supa FaiL **2**
OLD Lady's Revenge

Meet the creators:

K.T. likes to Hang out with her brothers.

Kip Likes computers and Quesadillas

Curly Likes Pizza and Frosting.

I THOUGHT YOU SAID YOUR COMIC WASN'T OFFENSIVE!

It wasn't.

The WHOLE WORLD GOT DESTROYED!

Billions of PeopLe Died!

Oh Yeah.

ALL because of A TooThPick?

I'm VERY **Disturbed** by these comics!!!

They're Just So **AWFUL!**

I thought they were **Supposed** to be awful!!!

How about You, Poppy?

I'll bet **YOU** made Something **Nice!**

I did, Daddy!!! It's called "The Cute, Little, Fluffy Cloud...

... of Death."

The Cute, Little, Fluffy Cloud of Death

by Poppy

Once there was a cute, little cloud.

She was fluffy and dead.

Hi

Hi

But the sun was mean to her.

HEY

You're creeping me out!!!

GO AWAY

So the cute, little, fluffy cloud of death cried and cried.

The End

about the author

Poppy is a Frog who Lives with her Family in a Camper by the Pond. She Likes Ghosts and Skeletons and drawing and Monsters and rain. She ~~likes~~ likes to draw every day because it is Fun. ALso, she likes Dogs.

the end.

Is anybody bullying you?

No.

Then why did you make that comic?

Oh. Because I like skeletons and ghosts and—

But why was the little cloud **DEAD?**

I don't know.

Lots of people are dead.

Hey! I'm back!

Just in time! We're giving out **AWARDS!**

Snip Snip

DiD I WiN?

Yep! You got the prize for Weirdest comic!!!

YAY!

And you guys get the award for **CRAZIEST** comic!

AWESOME!

And the Award for **MOST VIOLENTEST** comic Goes to...

SUPA FAIL!

yeSSSSSSS!

And here, Pedro. You win for the **GROSSEST** comic!

Sweet!

Let's get STARTED on The Sequel!

Let's make a comic About **POOP WARS!**

And we got an idea about **EviL ZOMBiES!**

I'm gonna make a story about a **DEAD AiRPLANE!**

I'll use felt, glue, and construction paper!

And I'm gonna make **DENNiS THe TOOTHBRUSH: DiNOSAUR LAWYeR 2!**

You should probably put some dinosaurs in it this time.

And also, maybe a **_PLOT_**!

Something should **HAPPEN** this time. I'm just sayin'.

I'VE GOT IT!!!

MURDER!!!

ALRIGHT, THAT'S ENOUGH!!!

CHAPTER 4

NEW RULES

FROM NOW ON, everyone's comics must be **WHOLESOME**...

...and **UPLIFTING**...

...with **GOOD VALUES** and **MORALS!!!**

What's the problem this time, FLIPPY?

It's my kids!!!

I think they're DISTURBED!!!

Where are they?

They're all downstairs in the bowling alley.

Oh.

Melvin

Poppy

But look at these comics they made!!!

They're filled with **ViOLENCE**...

... and **POTTY HUMOR**...

... and ...

... and ...

... and one of them is about **DEATH!**

OH, NO! WE MUST OPERATE AT ONCE!

HOLD YOUR HORSES, DOC!!!

Let's read these comics first!!!

swipe

Good idea, Nurse Lady!

And so...

Haw! Haw! He saved the toothpick!!!

SUPA FAIL

Well? Have you made a diagnosis yet?

Umm, uhhh... ... Hmmm...

I Think you're over-reacting again, Flippy!

OVER-REACTING?

But what about the **ViOLENCE?**

What about the **POTTY JOKES?**

What about the Reckless disregard for the Sanctity of Life and Stuff?

Dude, **THAT'S NORMAL!**

ADULTS make up stories about that stuff all the time...

... and we call them ARTISTS...

...and GENIUSES, and VISIONARIES!

Look at SHAKESPEARE:

It's all DEATH and VIOLENCE and FART JOKES!

Poot!

If it's **NORMAL** and **HEALTHY** for Grown-ups...

...then why not for **Kids**?

Are you seriously going to **PRAISE** a grown-up...

The Canterbury Tales by Chau

...and **SHAME** a child...

To Daddy From Pedro

...**FOR THE SAME DARN Thing?**

The Mysterious STRANGER by Mark Twa
The cute Little Fluff Clou De

Take a chill Pill, dude!!!

Maybe you're right.

I'm ALWAYS RIGHT!

Let's Go, Doctor!

Bye, Flippy!

I'll try to be more chill!!!

You Better!!!

Where did ya get all that **WISDOM**, Nurse Lady?

I have a degree in baby frog psychology.

Before you kids start your comic club today...

...I want to apologize.

I'm sorry if I discouraged you yesterday.

I shouldn't have let **MY TASTES** spoil everything.

You kids should write stories that make **YOU** happy.

Write things that make **YOU** laugh!

And try not to worry about what others think.

You'll never be able to please everyone anyway!

There will always be haters...

...So just focus on what **YOU** **LOVE**!

Do that...

... and you'll never fail.

Oh! oh! Ooh!!!

Yes, Melvin?

We should always do our best, though, Right?

Of course!

And we should try to **IMPROVE**, Right?

Absolutely!

Well, since **YOU** brought it up...

I made an **ALL-NEW, IMPROVED** comic last night!

Wanna Read it?

Certainly!!!

Dennis the Toothbrush who wanted to be a DINOSAUR Lawyer 2: Cretaceous Courtroom

By Melvin

One time there was a toothbrush named Dennis.

He went to Law School.

Law School

Soon, he was a Lawyer.

That was easy!

I want to help Dinosaurs with my mad Lawyer skills.

So he got in a Time machine

and went back 67 Million Years.

108

FUN FACTS about the cast

SPINOSAURUSES
Lived on Land and water. Their fins may have been used to heat up their body Quickly, or to Attract a mate.

Length: over 50 Feet ★ Weight: over 6 Tons ★ carnivore ★ Cretaceous Period

Triceratopses
were vegetarians that had 800 teeth. Their worst enemy was the T. Rex.

Length: up To 30 Feet ★ weight: up to 13 Tons ★ Cretaceous Period

IGuanoDons
had Five Fingers and could grasp things with their hands. Their Thumbs had big spikes on them. sweeeet!!!

★ Size: up to 43 Feet Long ★ Weight: over 8 Tons ★ Vegan ★ Cretaceous Period

Toothbrushes were invented in 1977 by Dr. William Brush. He named them after his daughter, "Toothetta". They are mainly used For oral hygiene and are not Known to practice Law.

Size: up to 10 inches ★ Weight: 6 ounces ★ Diet: PLAQue ★ Disco ERA To present

ABout the Genius Worker:

Coolest
Author
Award
of all-Time.
NO
TakebACKS

TootheTta
Brush
Memorial
Award.

Peel it,
sir
Prize
For
Literature

MeLvin the Frog is the multiPLe major award-winninG author and illustrator of over 1 Graphic novels.

Known throughout the globe for his intelligence and Dashing good Looks, MeLvin is also regarded as a Key influencer and a trend-setting Fashion guru.

How can one Frog be so Awesome? Scientists are Working around the clock to solve this mystery.

"The world may never Know," said the world's second-smartest person, Dr. Gene Yiss.

Fans and admirers of Melvin can purchase his autograph For $1.00 while supplies Last. Buy Ten, get the eleventh For 1/2 Price!!!

Very Good, Melvin!

Yeah! That was **WAY BETTER** than last time!

I told him to put Dinosaurs in it!!!

I WAS GOING TO ANYWAY!

And I'm not tryin' to **TATTLE** or anything, but...

I saw him **COPYING** how to draw out of a **BOOK**!!!

Yeah, but I WASN'T **TRACING!** I was just... I was...

It's okay to copy!

That's how I taught myself to draw!!!

Me too!

I started copying cartoon characters that I Liked...

...and I drew them over and over...

... and soon I was making up my **OWN** characters...

...in my **own** style!

But it all started with **COPYING!**

Ditto, dude!

See? It's OKAY to COPY!!!!

BLeeeah!

MELViN!

Oh, and one more thing:

You shouldn't make up "facts," buddy!

I DiDn't!

Toothbrushes were **NOT** invented in 1977!

Oh, yeah.

Well I **TRIED** to look it up...

...but Summer and Starla were hoggin' the computer all last night!!!

WE WERE WORKING!

Yeah! We were editing our HAIKU Photo-Comic!!!

Check it out!!!

BIRDS
FLOWERS
TREES

HAIKU AND
PHOTOS BY
SUMMER
AND
STARLA

Little flower buds
Even if no one can see
Open anyway

The ambitious crow.
We see a twig in her beak
but she sees a home

From a great distance
branches pierce the sapphire sky
like dark lightning bolts

but branches up close
will tell another story:
one of potential

If you look closely
you can find marvelous things
that yearn to be seen.

If you look closer
you might find something hidden
deep in the shadows.

Which of these are we?
Shall we hide or brightly shine?
We cannot do both

We are very small

but the things inside our hearts

could fill up the sky

About Haiku
by Summer & Starla

haiku are poems
with seventeen syllables
they come from Japan

the syllables are
divided into three lines
five, seven, and five

they tell stories of
nature and beauty and truth
simple and profound

even though haiku
may take decades to master
kids write the best ones

About the poet and the photographer:

Summer and Starla
are artists and BFFs
but they're sisters, first

Starla loves to read
to disappear in a book
to get lost in words

Summer dreams about
dinosaurs and String theory
She also loves crêpes

That was **WONDERFUL,** girls!

Thanks, Daddy!!!

We're gonna make a **NEW** Photo-comic this weekend!!!

Sweeeeet!!! You guys **RULE!**

Thanks! We know!

Does anybody else have a comic to share?

Nope.

No.

Not yet.

Well, tomorrow is our **LAST** club meeting this week...

...So everybody bring in your comics tomorrow!

But we're not done yet!

Us neither!

It doesn't matter! Just bring us a **SNEAK PREVIEW**...

...And we'll have a **COMIC CLUB SHOW AND TELL PARTY!!!**

HOORAY!!!

Soon...

Hey, what are you two still doing here???

Everyone else has gone to work on their comics.

We know. But...

...We **STILL** can't think up any ideas.

Yeah. We're still waiting to be **INSPIRED!**

You know, girls, I've always said:

"Those who sit around and **WAIT** for inspiration...

...don't **DESERVE** inspiration!"

Um—What does **That** mean?

It means **QUIT BEING LAZY!**

FORCE yourselves to create!!!

But we're not good at making up stories!

Then write something that's **TRUE!**

Write about **YOURSELVES!**

Make an **AUTO-BIOGRAPHICAL** comic!

Raine, you could write about your feelings...

...And Wendy, you could write about your adventures!!!

Wendy, you can't make an auto-biographical comic **ABOUT** **ME!**

Why?

Because he doesn't drive a car, silly!

Oh, yeah!

No— That's not why

OKAY, DADDY...

Tell us **EVErythinG** about your life!!!

Yeah! Start at the **Beginning!**

Well, okay— it all started a long time ago...

CHAPTER 8

The Show and Tell Party

The next day...

Well, we've come to the end of our **First week!**

So Let's PARTY! YAY! YAY!

PARTY Time

HOORAY!!!

I made Monster cheese sandwiches for everybody!!!

And I can draw faces on them if you want!!!

MUSTAR

Ketchup

And I made **DOG Poo Brownies!**

They're just regular brownies...

...but I rolled them into little balls...

... then squeezed them toGether!!!

Mmmm! They're **DiSGUStingLY DeLicious!!!**

Be more chill...
...be more chill...
...be more chill...

And **we** baked a SUPA FAIL CAKE!

WhUH!

FRAPK

HOLD UP!

Poink

CAKE POPS! Get Your Cake Pops Right Here!!!

Mmmmm! Grassy!!!

Li'l Petey and I will Go first with our sneak Peek of:

SQUID Kid and KATYDID!

What's a Katydid?

It's like a cricket.

oh.

I knew that!

So without further ado...

🎵 Ta-Daaa! 🎵

SQUID KID AND KATYDID

An epic sneak Preview
by Molly and Li'l Petey

In a world...

...Where everyone looks the same...

One kid looked different than the rest.

And so...

Get Lost, Squid Kid!

Yeah! Scram!

Boo-Hoo Hoo!!!

But Watch out, world...

...because when these two misfits meet...

...Things will never be the same!!!

ZZ-ZZ

BFF's FoReveR!!

SQUID KID and KATYDID

WoRLD's GReatest Misfits

Coming Soon!

We made a preview, too!

It's about Daddy...

...and the life he lived **BEFORE** he met us!

Daddy had a life before us?

No way!

Yeah! It's **TRUE!** And we're telling his story!!!

Check out this **SNEAK PEEK!!!**

Baby Flippy

A Sneak Peek by
Wendy and Raine

Wendy and Raine proudly present:

A True Story of Courage.

Baby Flippy

Before he was Daddy...

...he was *DINNER!*

COMING SOON

to a Cat Kid Comic Club near you!

We don't want Baby FLiPPY to get killed!

Now, now...

I didn't get killed when I was a baby!

I'm here now, aren't I ???

Oh, yeah.

That means that everything worked out okay in the end.

Gee, thanks for the **SPOILERS,** Daddy!

Yeah! Now we know the **ENDING!!!**

SLAP!

Does anybody else have a sneak peek?

WE DO, DADDY!

We took pictures of our action figures...

...and we're making a comic with them!

155

CHUBBS MᶜSPiDERBUTT

An Epic Preview by The Hacker Bros.

In a world...

... where sinister scoundrels...

... Subjugate the souls of civilization,

HAW
HAW
HAW!

A dude accidentally sat on a spider.

plop!

OWie!!!

...and the butt of a spider!

CHUBBS McSPIDERBUTT

An Epic Photo-Comic by
The H.A.C.K.E.R. Brothers
(Heroic Alpha Commando Kids: Elite Regiment)

STARRING

Zeus Goldberg
as
Chubbs
McSpiderbutt

Wei Chan
as
Jake the
Flying Spider

Brock Manhammer
as
Dr. Pasty
McSprinkles

And
Introducing
Scott the Worm
as
Scott the Worm

COMING SOON

That was very good, boys...

...but I don't Understand...

...How did all of your action figures get broken?

Oh. Because we threw 'em off the—

They broke all by themselves by accident.

Alright, would anyone else like to share their preview?

We would, Daddy!

We're making a comic with clay and cardboard and stuff!

I wrote the story...

...And we made the art!

BABY FROG SQUAD

Story By: Billie

Art by: Frida, EL, and Deb

Once upon a time...

...there were three baby frogs...

...who went to the Police Academy.

They studied hard...

... learned Kung-fu...

... and directed lots of traffic!

But soon, they got tired of working for the man!

Soon, a bully was detected on planet #39.

Let's Go!

And So...

RAAAR!!!

HEY! Quit bullying that little dude!!!

MAKE ME!!!

I don't make Cupcakes!

I eat 'em for **BREAKFAST!**

Who will win the epic space Battle?

Find out in...

BABY FROG SQUAD

COMING SOON!

That was **WONDERFUL!**

Thanks, Daddy!

Yeah! You all did an **AWESOME** job this week!!!

I can't believe that **EVERYBODY** made a comic!!!

Actually, I made **TWO** comics!!!

Two **AWARD-WINNING** comics!

I thought you were trying to be more chill, Daddy.

Do you need to sit on the time-out rock?

I—I'm sorry I yelled at you, kids.

Don't worry, Daddy!

It's just like we learned this week:

And so...

Welp, you can't ask for a sweeter ending than **THAT!**

... or a **SAPPIER** one !!!

Don't Miss our **NEXT EPIC ADVENTURE!**

CAT KID COMIC CLUB

BOOK 2 COMING SOON!

NOTES & FUN FACTS

⭐ Chubbs McSpiderbutt was made from a broken action figure, epoxy putty, enamel paint, and 48 black pipe cleaners (chenille stems) twisted together to make his legs.

⭐ The robot bully in BABY FROG SQUAD was made out of cardboard, hot glue, tape, paper clips, and plastic salad dressing lids (for the eyeballs).

⭐ The baby frogs in BABY FROG SQUAD were made with Japanese rice clay (eyes, bodies, hands, and feet) and toothpicks painted with acrylics and markers (limbs and eyelashes).

⭐ The pencils on page 164 are toothpicks colored with markers.

⭐ Summer and Starla's poetic description of haiku on page 125 is NOT definitive. The art of haiku is ever-evolving and has a rich, complex history. English-language haiku first appeared in the late 19th century. They were based on Japanese poems called renga, which were structured, improvised verse poetry collaborations, often performed live. The first stanza of a renga, called the hokku, became what we commonly think of as haiku.

⭐ One of the oldest and most famous Japanese haiku (technically a hokku) has a frog in it.

> Breaking the silence
> Of an ancient pond,
> A frog jumped into the water—
> A deep resonance.

> —Bashō (1644-1694)
> Translated by
> Nobuyuki Yuasa

GET READING
WITH DAV PILKEY!

ABOUT THE
AUTHOR-ILLUSTRATOR

When Dav Pilkey was a kid, he was diagnosed with ADHD and dyslexia. Dav was so disruptive in class that his teachers made him sit out in the hallway every day. Luckily, Dav loved to draw and make up stories. He spent his time in the hallway creating his own original comic books — the very first adventures of Dog Man and Captain Underpants.

In college, Dav met a teacher who encouraged him to illustrate and write. He won a national competition in 1986 and the prize was the publication of his first book, WORLD WAR WON. He made many other books before being awarded the 1998 California Young Reader Medal for DOG BREATH, which was published in 1994, and in 1997 he won the Caldecott Honor for THE PAPERBOY.

THE ADVENTURES OF SUPER DIAPER BABY, published in 2002, was the first complete graphic novel spin-off from the Captain Underpants series and appeared at #6 on the USA Today bestseller list for all books, both adult and children's, and was also a New York Times bestseller. It was followed by THE ADVENTURES OF OOK AND GLUK: KUNG FU CAVEMEN FROM THE FUTURE and SUPER DIAPER BABY 2: THE INVASION OF THE POTTY SNATCHERS, both USA Today bestsellers. The unconventional style of these graphic novels is intended to encourage uninhibited creativity in kids.

His stories are semi-autobiographical and explore universal themes that celebrate friendship, tolerance, and the triumph of the good-hearted.

Dav loves to kayak in the Pacific Northwest with his wife.